THE BEST THINGS IN LIFE ARE FREE

THE BEST THINGS IN LIFE ARE FREE

C. T. FRANKLIN

Copyright © 2014 by C. T. Franklin.

Library of Congress Control Number: 2014909049
ISBN: Hardcover   978-1-4990-8641-6
           Softcover   978-1-4990-8629-4
           eBook   978-1-4990-8630-0

All rights reserved. No part of this book may be reproduced or transmitted in any form or by any means, electronic or mechanical, including photocopying, recording, or by any information storage and retrieval system, without permission in writing from the copyright owner.

This is a work of fiction. Names, characters, places and incidents either are the product of the author's imagination or are used fictitiously, and any resemblance to any actual persons, living or dead, events, or locales is entirely coincidental.

Any people depicted in stock imagery provided by Thinkstock are models, and such images are being used for illustrative purposes only.
Certain stock imagery © Thinkstock.

This book was printed in the United States of America.

Rev. date: 07/26/2014

To order additional copies of this book, contact:
Xlibris LLC
0-800-056-3182
www.xlibrispublishing.co.uk
Orders@xlibrispublishing.co.uk

CONTENTS

INTRODUCTION 11

CHAPTER 1. THE FREE GIFT 13

CHAPTER 2. THE GIFT OF LIFE 17

CHAPTER 3. THE GIFT OF FRIENDSHIP 21

CHAPTER 4. THE GIFT OF LOVE....................... 27

CHAPTER 5. THE GIFT OF GIFTS 33

CHAPTER 6. THE GIFT OF MUSIC..................... 39

This book is dedicated to all the wonderful people who seek to make a beneficial difference in the lives of those around them.

A letter from Mudsy

Hello, boys and girls,

I love to have fun, and every day I look for something to play with. I sometimes sneak some of Mikey's socks and hide them. It makes me happy when I see him looking through his drawers or under his bed or even in the downstairs cupboard. Eventually, when I know he has had enough, I bark to where I have hidden them. I just love it when I see that big smile on his face and when Mikey chases me around the garden. I am so happy to have a lovely home and someone who cares for me.

Will you help me make the children happy? It would be lovely to see and hear the children playing in the play area built so that mummies and daddies can have some special time as a family. What big smiles would be seen on the little children's faces. Please sell as many copies of this book as you can and be a part of something big. A *big* hug from Mudsy.

Introduction

Mikey was upset at the death of his auntie. It made him sad and lonely. He had so many questions about life and had no answers. He never met his dad, and his mum was so busy working to give him all the things that she never had. One day he found a puppy that had been abandoned. He took it home and poured his love and attention on it. Soon things would change for Mikey. Life took a turn of events that no one would have predicted. His life became exciting. He would learn how strong he could be and began to face life with its ups and downs with feelings of hope and happiness.

The Free Gift

'I'm bored, bored, bored,' Mikey grumbled to himself as he walked, hands in his pockets and head bowed down. 'Summer holidays are so boring now. They used to be so good when Auntie Kate was here. We used to do baking together, have water fights when the weather was good. Sometimes we would meet Auntie's friend Joan, and they would spend the day together. Auntie always made a picnic lunch that would water your mouth just thinking about it. Sometimes we would go to Tittesworth, where Auntie would unfold the picnic rug, place it carefully down on the grass, and proceed to open the picnic basket. While Auntie and Joan talked—and boy, did they talk, they would talk the hind legs off a donkey—I would go to the playground and always made some new friends to play with.'

'I loved those times,' said Mikey to himself with a tear in his eye as the warm glow of his auntie's embrace melted away all his fears and troubles.

Mikey was sad thinking about his auntie; nothing made sense any more to him. Life seemed so complicated at the moment. Sometimes he dreamt he was in a jungle and, on many occasions, would wake up sweating and fearful as he could not find his way out. He had no one now to talk to; now Auntie was gone. He felt so alone. Mum was always busy and never seemed to have time for him, not the way his precious auntie had. He never knew his dad, and he often wondered what he looked like. He could not ask his mum as she would always say the same thing, 'Good riddance to him.'

Life seemed so unfair. His mum had no time for him, his dad was gone, and above all, the big C (cancer) had taken his precious auntie away from him. Since his auntie died, he often asked the questions, 'Who am I?' 'What am I doing here?' 'What is life all about?' This made Mikey so angry that he kicked a tin can straight across to the other side of the road.

'Hemmem,' heard Mikey as the tin can landed on what Mikey thought was a heap of rubbish. Mikey went over to investigate. There before his eyes lay a puppy. A sad injured, dirty puppy; a puppy which looked starved and had a damaged right eye. Mikey stood there in shock. How long had the puppy been there? he thought. Had no one seen it, or did they purposely keep on walking? Did he not himself see a priest go by and a businessman with a briefcase? Now he understood why they walked quickly by this patch of the path. 'How could they leave you like this?' said Mikey softly to the puppy as he bent down and cradled him in his arms.

'I won't leave you here. I'll bring you home and ask Mum to help me take care of you. Don't you worry now,' said Mikey, still in his soft tone of voice so as not to frighten the puppy. Mikey put the puppy inside his jacket to help him keep warm and headed home.

'What have you found now?' said Mikey's mum in a stern voice as Mikey entered the front door. Mikey was always finding things. One day, while near a golf course, Mikey found about ten golf balls. He brought them into the office and was paid some money for them. Another time, he found a camera. Sadly, there was no charger and the camera got wet in the rain, so he never got it to work. Another time, he found a mirror from a motorbike. This was his treasured possession as he thought one day he would buy a motorbike and go so fast on the road that the very hairs on his neck would stand up.

As Mikey stood hesitantly by the door, the little puppy whimpered in pain and hunger. Mikey opened his jacket, hoping that his mum's reaction would be one of pity. 'Please, please, please, Mum, can we look after him? I'll do the washing up every night and make my bed and keep my room tidy, only please can we keep him and look after him? He has no one else.' Mikey's mum took one look at the puppy and Mikey's pleading eyes, threw her hands in the air, and turned on her heel and walked off in defeat.

That evening, Mikey gave the puppy some food and a bath and put a covering on the puppy's damaged right eye. As Mikey lay in his bed that night, he wondered what to call his newfound friend. His newfound friend looked at Mikey, and Mikey looked at his newfound friend, and suddenly something magical happened between them. A bond so strong drew them both together. It felt to Mikey that they had been together from the very beginning of time. Surely, it was meant to be that they met in such circumstances. As Mikey and his newfound friend snuggled together, a name came to Mikey. 'I'll call you Mudsy because I have taken you out of the mud.' And as Mikey dozed off, the words from his auntie Kate came into his mind, 'The best things in life are free.'

'True, true,' whispered Mikey sleepily to himself. 'I could never afford to pay for a puppy and such a magical feeling I had when I connected with my newfound friend.' It was better than any magical book or film that he had seen, and it was all free.

And so the first day drifted into night, and soon Mikey was sound asleep. *Zzzz.*

The Gift of Life

Mikey woke up with a start. What time was it? How did he sleep so late? This was the first time in ages that he slept without disturbing dreams, and it felt so good. He looked to see where Mudsy was. Ah, there he was, faithful as ever by his bed, waiting for him to wake up.

Mikey went to see what the weather was up to. As he looked out the window, elbows bent and resting on the windowpane, face in the palms of his hands, he thought of how very changeable the weather was lately. Sometimes he felt very changeable inside. He thought, one time he was angry with life, another time he was sad about his life, another time he was frustrated, all in one day. As he went to the wardrobe to get his clothes, he nearly tripped over something. While Mikey was asleep, Mudsy became bored and decided to investigate what was under the bed. He found some trainers. They were pushed so far under the bed that it took a long time for him to get them out. 'Where did you find these?' Mikey gasped. 'I haven't worn those since Auntie Kate di—' The sadness came upon him like a flood. Auntie Kate loved running for charity. Her favourite one was the Samaritans, and she raised thousands of pounds for them. He thought he might run one day like his auntie, and he asked his mum for a pair of trainers. Mum bought him the best of trainers and also some running gear. Mum was like that. All he had to do was to ask, and she always bought him the very best of stuff to the envy of his schoolmates.

'Oh, okay, I suppose you want to go for a walk,' Mikey said to Mudsy. Mikey put aside his sadness and put on his trainers. He would do this only for his Mudsy. It was a hard thing for Mikey to run again; it brought back memories. However, as Mikey ran with Mudsy by his side, it wasn't the sad memories that came into his mind—it was the happy ones. As he ran, something inside him changed. He remembered his teacher Mr Stevens and how he taught him about the butterfly. Mr Stevens said the butterfly is first a caterpillar. Then it goes through metamorphosis, and then it is changed into a beautiful butterfly. He remembered the story his teacher told of a person who felt sorry for the caterpillar and could not bear to see it struggling in its cocoon that he snipped the cocoon to help the caterpillar. However, when the butterfly emerged from the cocoon, it could not fly as its wings were not strong enough.

'The butterfly needed to struggle inside its cocoon. This struggle helps to develop its wings,' said Mr Stevens. 'How sad for the butterfly,' thought Mikey. 'It won't be able to fly away if a cat comes near.' Mikey wondered about his life. Did his struggles make him strong? Suddenly, out of nowhere, he had a desire to become strong, and for once, he was thankful for his life. Truly, he thought, since Mudsy came into his life, things were getting better every day.

Mikey arrived home. His mum was out shopping. They were both very hungry after their run. Mikey gave Mudsy his favourite dish, and he had a bowl of cornflakes. They were both full of energy, and Mikey started to chase after Mudsy and vice versa. They were having great fun when suddenly they knocked the table, and the large packet of cornflakes scattered all over the floor. 'I better clean this up before Mum gets back,' thought Mikey. Mikey got the vacuum out and cleaned up the cornflakes. He had so much energy that he vacuumed the whole floor and the stairs without even thinking about it. 'I'll do the dishes and put them away,' he said to Mudsy. When he had finished, he went up to his room with Mudsy following close to his heels. 'This room is very untidy,' Mikey thought to himself and started to put away his things. 'Nay, on the other hand, it's just the way I like it, a tidy mess.' He laughed to himself.

On arriving home, his mum let out a cry of delight. Mikey ran down the stairs. Had Mum received a parcel in the post, or did they have a visitor? What made her cry out in delight? Nothing had arrived. There was only Mum sitting at the table. She opened her purse, said nothing, and handed Mikey a £5 note. Mikey took the money and politely gave his mum a kiss on the cheek. It must have pleased his mum to see the house clean. Grown-ups, he'd never understand them. He would have preferred a big hug from his mum. But was he mistaken? Did he see a small tear in the corner of his mum's eye? Mikey went to the shop to spend his money and bought some treats for Mudsy and himself to have a night feast.

That night, as they both lay on the bed, Mikey spoke to Mudsy like you would a friend. Although Mudsy could not talk back, Mikey just knew by the way that he looked at him with his one brown eye that Mudsy understood everything he said. Mikey talked about how his mum's purpose in life was to work hard so he could have the very best of everything. His auntie Kate's life was to help others.

Maybe one day he would find his purpose in life. As he dozed off, the words of his auntie's song rang in his ears. 'Run, run, run, get those happy hormones working. Run, run, ruuun.' Soon Mikey fell fast asleep. *Zzzzzz.*

The Gift of Friendship

Mikey woke up to the pitter-patter of the raindrops falling on the rooftop. 'What a miserable day,' he thought as he looked at Mudsy. 'What will we do today?' He knew Mudsy needed his walk, so after breakfast, he put on his wellies and rain jacket and headed off for a long walk with Mudsy. As Mikey walked, a lady with shopping bags in both hands, her hair drenched with the rain, stopped to ask Mikey what happened to the dog's eye. This happened many times when he was with Mudsy. Before, when he walked down the road on his own, it seemed as if he was invisible—nobody noticed him. Now many people wanted to hear the story of Mudsy, and Mikey would only be delighted to tell it. It was nice to have people being kind.

Mikey noticed a familiar face not far away. It was Wazer. What was he doing? He looked lost. Wazer saw Mikey heading for him. 'What's up, mate?' said Mikey. 'Are you not playing football today?' Wazer was football crazy. Any chance he had, he was out on the street knocking for his mates to come out to play. Sometimes his mates were not finished with their dinner, but Wazer would hang around waiting. 'Nobody wants to play because of the weather,' said Wazer with a low, downcast tone in his voice. 'Never mind,' said Mikey. 'Come along with us. We are going to our secret cave.'

'What happened to the dog?' said Wazer. 'What's the patch for?'

Mikey told him the story of how he found Mudsy.

'Wait a minute,' said Wazer. 'I have a hankie in my pocket that my mum gave to me that will match the patch.' Wazer put his hand in his pocket and took out a hankie—the same colour as the patch and the same matching dots—and proceeded to put it around Mudsy's neck.

'Hey up,' said Mikey. 'I don't want any snotty hankie around *my* dog's neck.'

'Na,' said Wazer. 'It's clean. I only took it from my mum to please her. It was her dad's. You see, he worked in the silk mills in Macclesfield. We have lots of them at home. They're too posh and silky for me.'

On and on the three of them walked, passing the old ruin across the stream up the bank. Soon they stopped.

'Where is this secret cave then?' said Wazer. 'I don't see any cave.'

'Take a look up there,' said Mikey.

Wazer looked up to where Mikey was pointing, and sure enough, he saw the cave. 'Wow, what a find,' said Wazer. 'Let's get in quickly out of this rain.' Up they climbed and entered the cave. 'Awesome bigger than it looks a luvy/lovely cave,' exclaimed Wazer. 'Look at this,' cried Wazer. 'Someone has collected sticks. Let's light a fire and get warm and dry.'

'We have no matches,' said Mikey.

'Shush, listen,' said Wazer 'I hear a sound. Don't make a move.' They sat waiting in silence. Suddenly, out of nowhere, they heard twigs being trampled on, and a voice with an unfamiliar accent bellowed into the cave, 'Anyone there?'

Too frightened to answer, they waited, hoping he would go away.

'Hiya, lads, wha' ye up to? It's a dirty day out there. This is the best place to be, a luvy cave all to ourselves,' spoke the chap all in one breath. To their horror, in came a tall lanky chap with hair down to his shoulders and a haversack on his back. 'Don't mind if I join ya?' he said as he made himself comfortable on the floor. They didn't have time to answer 'Well, we do' when Mudsy went over to him and was wagging his tail profusely. He liked the chap very much and didn't have any fear. 'Me name is Fredrick, but you can call me Freddy, and I'm from Dublin. I'm over here in me cousin's house for a while till everything settles down. Me ma died, you see, very suddenly, and everything is topsy-turvy. I had to get out of the house. It was doin' me head in.' Mikey held out his hand to shake Freddy's hand. He knew what it was like to lose someone close to him. *If Mudsy likes him, I'll make an effort to like him as well*, he thought.

'What's in the bag?' asked Wazer, not knowing why he asked.

'It's me music,' said Freddy and proceeded to open the haversack. Freddy took pages and pages out, all with music and words written on them.

'What kind of music do you write?' asked Wazer. He never knew anyone personally who sang, never mind wrote songs.

'Here, let me show you,' said Freddy as he put his hand into his haversack and took out a tin whistle. Freddy was about to play when he uttered, 'It's freezing here, let's light a fire.'

'We've no matches,' said both boys together.

'Not a bother,' said Freddy. 'Watch this.' Freddy put the twigs together, got two stones, and got the fire started in no time. 'Me granddad taught me that trick, and he learned it from his da'. He was Jewish, you see, and many times had to flee to safety with only the clothes on his back.'

'That's a coincidence,' said Mikey. 'My grandfather was Jewish too.'

Freddy began to play his music. 'I Don't Like Mondays' was one of them. The boys joined in. Suddenly Freddy stopped playing, Mikey stopped singing, and Freddy and Mikey both looked at each other, and at the same time, both fixed their eyes on Wazer.

'I never knew you could sing like that,' exclaimed Mikey.

'Wow, what a voice,' said Freddy. 'How did ya hit those high notes? What did ya have for breakfast?'

Wazer was just as surprised as anyone, and all three of them laughed until their sides ached. Even Mudsy joined in the fun, wagging his tail and giving the lads great big sloppy licks on their faces. The boys sat around the fire, singing and talking about their lives and putting the world to rights until the fire went out. It was now time to go. They parted friends and vowed to keep the friendship burning and made a time and day to meet again.

'What an adventurous, great day we had today, with lots of fun and laughter,' said Mikey to Mudsy as he giggled and playfully tickled Mudsy on his belly. 'I thought it was going to be miserable because of the rain, but if it wasn't raining, I would never have talked to Wazer. He would have been too busy playing football. We would not have met Freddy.' Mikey contemplated on how two people of the same gender and age who lived miles apart could have so much in common. Surely, it's a small, small world.

As Mikey was dozing off to sleep, he had a dream. He was holding his auntie's hand, and they were laughing together. The place where they were was very peaceful and beautiful. All the streets were made of gold. There were lots and lots of children there. Everyone was laughing. No tears were seen there. He felt so happy there that he wanted to stay. He was just about to ask if he could when his auntie turned to him, cupped his face in her hands, and spoke in a soft, gentle voice, 'Not yet. You have work to do below. When the time is right, I'll be waiting for you.' *Zzzzzzz.*

The Gift of Love

'How do I get out of here? How do I get out of here? There's no light.' Mikey was scared out of his wits. He was in the jungle trying to find a way out. He tried to call for help, but no words came out of his mouth. Suddenly something from behind jumped on him. His face became wet with sweat. 'Get off, get off,' he screeched. He jumped out of the way quickly and woke up to find himself on the floor near his bed and Mudsy licking his face. He was shaking all over. It was a long time since he had that dream. He thought it was gone forever, and here it was back again to haunt him. He looked at the clock by his bed. It was 4 a.m.

He went downstairs for a drink, and to his surprise, his mum was sitting at the table. She looked as if she had been crying. Mikey saw that on the table were a pile of bills. Mikey got a drink of milk from the fridge. He did not know what to say. He was going to say 'What's the matter, Mum?' but out of his mouth came the words 'I love you, Mum'. His mum looked at Mikey over her glasses and said in a strong, soft voice, 'I love you too, son.' Mikey went back to bed, holding those precious words in his heart. He had noticed that Mum was at home more than usual. He drank his glass of milk and snuggled back in bed.

'What was that?' yelled Mikey. He jumped out of bed. He had heard a big crash. He ran downstairs and found his mum on the floor. Panic was taking over him. He then heard himself talking sternly to himself, 'This is no time to panic. You know what to do. Just do it!' Mikey did know what to do. He had learned first aid in school. In an emergency, ring 999, and that was just what he did. 'Please come quickly, my mum's not well. She has collapsed.' The lady at the other end of the phone told him to stay on the phone after he had given the necessary details. She took Mikey step by step on what next to do. He would see if his mum was responding to his voice, then would place his two hands on top of each other in the centre of her chest and give thirty chest compressions. The lady was praising him all the time, which helped him immensely and gave him confidence. The doorbell rang. Mikey ran to it, opened the door, and let the ambulance crew in.

'Well done, lad, well done. We'll take over now,' said the crew. Mikey watched as they put the defibrillator on his mum's chest, and within two minutes, his mum was responding. The neighbour next door, Mrs Franklin, had seen the ambulance and came in to see if she could help. His mum went to the hospital, and Mrs Franklin stayed with Mikey until other arrangements were made.

It was hard for Mikey to see his mum on the bed, looking so frail. He was flabbergasted at the number of people who gave him high fives and claps on the back. 'Well done, lad. Great job. You saved your mum.' The headlines on the local Macclesfield newspaper said, 'YOUNG BOY SAVES HIS MUM BY GIVING HER CPR.'

He went to his mum's side. He had to be strong now. He had to become the man of the house, not the young child any more. The doctor came to see his mum. 'You had a very close call there, Mrs Sweet. You need to take it easy and have more rest. This young man will look after you. Won't you, son?' the doctor said.

'I'll do my best,' Mikey replied.

'And that's all you can do, only your best,' said the nurse standing by. She did not want Mikey to be too burdened as he was only a young boy.

'Mum, I don't need all the expensive things you buy for me,' Mikey said. 'I only want you. Do you remember last Christmas you bought me a great big Dr Who Voc Robot. To be quite honest, Mum, I got tired of it after a while, and I made a great big spaceship with the box. I really enjoyed making that, it was so much fun.' All the visitors laughed out loud. 'When I grow up, I'll have a great job, and I'll buy you a Rolls-Royce Phantom.' His mum put her frail arms around her son and held him so close he could hardly take a breath in.

Teresa, his mum's workmate, proceeded to tell a story. It was a Christmas Day, and she and her husband decided to go for a walk after the big feast. Three girls were playing with a supermarket shopping trolley in their garden. One of them was sitting in it, and the other two were pushing her. They were having great fun. Teresa asked them what presents they had for Christmas. They held out their hands and started to name them one by one, counting them on their fingers. 'And you are all playing with a shopping trolley and having great fun,' said Teresa to them. This caused an uproar of laughter among them so much so that the nurse asked them to be quiet. 'Laughter is a good medicine. We should laugh more,' said Teresa.

'Your uncle Philip is coming back from the army today, and he will be taking care of you until I come home,' his mum told Mikey.

Mikey met with his friends at the same time and place as before. After their high fives and strong handgrips, they sat down. Mikey told them all about his day's adventure. It was nice that they were together just chilling and singing.

'Yoo-hoo yoo-hoo called a very posh voice from outside the cave.

'Oh no,' exclaimed Freddy. 'It's me cousin busy Lizzie. She must have followed me here today. What a mess, and there was nowhere to hide.'

'What are you boys doing in here?'

'Hiya, Lizzie,' said Freddy, pretending to be happy to see her.

'My name is not Lizzie. It's Elizabeth, and well, you know it, you rascal,' exclaimed Elizabeth, with her hands on both hips. 'Mum asked me to look after you, and I take my job very seriously—very seriously indeed.'

'Well, this cave is only for boys, and we are conducting our business at the mo,' said Wazer, hoping she would go away, and the sooner the better, he thought.

'Excuse me,' exclaimed Elizabeth in her nice, posh accent. 'Don't think you can easily push me away. One day I will be in a very high position. You all will do what I want you to do. I'm no pushover,' she protested.

Mikey sat in silence and awe at the sight before his eyes. Lizzie, or Elizabeth (he better get used to calling her by her proper name in case he got a scolding), was only four feet tall and about twelve years old. She wore very posh clothes, and her perfume filled the cave. She spoke with authority. 'When I come back here, I will bring my little sister, and you better let us in on your business,' she said indignantly. She turned on her heels and walked off.

Mikey sat in his bed that night reading. He missed his mum. 'When would it all go back to normal?' he thought. He was at the part in the book where the pirates had captured a girl and held her for ransom. When he looked into the face of the girl, it was Elizabeth's face. She had her hands on her hips, demanding to be set free. With one swift turn of her heels, she got away, leaving only the smell of her perfume in his nostrils. The smell went down into his whole body, and he felt he was on cloud nine. *Zzzzzzzzzzz.*

The Gift of Gifts

This morning Mikey woke up with an excitement in his spirit. 'I feel that there is something special going to happen today,' he thought. He rummaged through his drawers to find something nice to wear. That morning he made sure to wash behind his ears, brush his hair, and clean his teeth. He went downstairs. A man in an army uniform was sitting at the table. He introduced himself. 'I'm your uncle Philip,' he said. 'I am going to take care of you until your mum is better.' Mikey didn't remember his uncle. He had been in the army for many years and didn't come home much, and when he did, Mikey had been on holidays, so their paths never met. But here he was now in his living room. Mikey noticed that his uncle had only one arm; the other one was artificial. He also had a scar on the right side of his face. *He's been in the wars*, thought Mikey.

'Here, son,' said Uncle Philip. 'I brought you some souvenirs from the war.' Uncle Philip put his hand in his pocket and took out a brown paper parcel tied with a string, and gave it to Mikey. He thanked his uncle and untied the string and opened the parcel. He put the contents of the parcel on the table. Here were treasures any boy would love to have. There were buttons from an army coat. Uncle Philip told Mikey the story of the buttons. They were from the coat of his best mate who was killed in action. He and his best mate were together when suddenly, out of what seemed nowhere, shots were fired. They ran for cover, but he had been wounded, and his friend tried to pull him to safety. His best mate was shot while saving him. He survived, but his arm had to be amputated. His best mate had four children. Uncle Philip's sadness was clearly seen on his face. He felt sorry not for his own grief but for the children left without a daddy. He wished he could do something for them. On the table were some badges, a buckle from a belt, and a small Gideon's Bible with a bullet still in it. 'This little book saved my life,' said Uncle Philip. That bullet should have gone through my heart, but this little book took the blow.

'Thank you very much. I will take good care of them and always treasure them.' Mikey gave his uncle Philip a handshake. He was proud of him and told him so.

He couldn't wait to show Mudsy and his newfound friends his treasures.

In the cave, he opened the parcel and laid each item carefully on the ground. He told his uncle's stories. The boys were fascinated and wished that they too could have treasures like these.

'Yoo-hoo yoo-hoo' came a familiar posh voice. 'I told you I'd be back, and this is my little sister, Annie.' Mikey quickly took his treasures from the ground and was just about to wrap them up when they caught Elizabeth's eye. 'What are they, and what business are you conducting?' she exclaimed. The boys sat flabbergasted, unable to utter a word. 'Well?' Elizabeth waited for an answer.

To break the silence, Mikey spoke first. 'We were just wondering what we could do to help children whose daddies have been killed in the war,' replied Mikey, not knowing what to say next and hoping his mates would say something as well.

'Splendid, splendid indeed, I will make my stand for the children who lost their parents fighting in the war. Let's get down to business right away,' said Elizabeth.

Wazer and Freddy looked at each other, put their palms up, and uttered, 'Whatever.'

They made a pact and placed their left hand one on top of the other and then their right hand. 'Well, are you going to stay this way all day?' exclaimed Elizabeth to Mikey as his hand was on top of Elizabeth's. How long it was there, he did not know. It seemed like forever. The cave—once a place of fun, music, singing, and relaxing—was now the busiest place ever as ideas were discussed and plans made to help children in need.

It was all settled then; they would do a concert and talent competition.

Sophia had a friend in school whose parents had a very large back garden. Her job was to ask Jamie's mum permission to use the garden. Maybe his brothers, Winston and Natanael, would help as well. Winston was gifted with making things. He could build the stage. Natanael was gifted with computer skills. He would put it on YouTube and Facebook. Jamie was skilled in photography. 'We could get some great photos and sell them on eBay,' she said to Jamie. Their mum, Dawn, was gifted with baking skills. She might bake some cakes, and they could sell them to get some money as well. Annie loved helping people. She was born to do this, she thought.

Mikey's job was to organise the event. He would be the director and give everyone a job to do. 'And they better do it well.' He made it known very clearly—very clearly indeed. He was also going to do a double act with his Mudsy. They would be called Mopsy and Mudsy. Mikey thought that Mudsy was so talented that he could get him to ride a bike. Mikey loved a challenge.

Freddy's job was to get as many of his musical friends to play at the concert as he could. He would form a band and call it the Rat-a-tat-tats. He would be able to play all his own songs. *How mind-blowing is that?* he thought.

Wazer's job was to sing. However, he had better get to learn some songs not only for young people but for their mums and dads as well.

Last but not least was Elizabeth's job. This job needed someone strong in spirit. They would keep up the morale of everyone who was taking part. They would try to keep the peace so that there would be no falling out, and lead the team on so that they would finish what they had started. They would make sure that everyone was using their gifts and none was left out. This job was fit for a queen, and it was unanimous that Elizabeth was the very person for the job. And so the work began.

Mikey got home a little later than usual. He was so excited about the project that when he saw his uncle, he blurted everything out to him. His uncle was so impressed that children wanted to help other children in need. He had an idea himself for the concert. He did not say anything but was keeping it as a surprise.

Mikey was exhausted by the time it was bedtime. How life had changed for him, he thought. First, Mudsy came into his life and had been a faithful friend ever since. He thought about how his life was sad and boring, but now he was enjoying his life with all his newfound friends. They were people from different parts of the world, but they had lots of things in common.

He remembered his mum in the hospital. How he used to take her for granted, but no more, he thought. Then there was Elizabeth. 'I think she likes me,' he thought. He did catch her taking a sly glance at him when she thought he wasn't looking. 'We could become the very best of mates,' he hoped. And then there was the concert. It was going to be a success. It had to be for the sake of the children in need. That night, Mikey knelt down at the side of his bed, put his hands together, bowed his head, and said a prayer. Getting up, he said to Mudsy, 'We must sleep now, we have a big day ahead of us—a very big day indeed.' *Zzzzzzz*.

The Gift of Music

Mikey woke up to the sound of music playing in his ears. It was Saturday, the big day, the day of the concert. Mikey had lots of thoughts swimming around in his brain. He was the main man. All the responsibility was on his shoulders. Everyone depended on him to have direction and push for outstanding results. 'I'll make sure everyone pulls their weight. There will be no room for failure,' he thought. Having this responsibility seemed to have toughened Mikey up. He was very soft on the inside but needed to be tough on the outside. He would make sure everyone knew for definite that he was no mug.

Panic struck his little heart. He heard the pitter-patter of the raindrops on the windowpane. He sighed. His mind went back to the time when he met his friends. It was raining then. Suddenly hope sprang into his heavy heart. 'There'll be no clouds in our hearts today,' he told Mudsy. Rain or no rain, the show must go on.'

'See you soon, Uncle Philip,' he shouted.

'Cheers. See you later, son,' he replied with a playful grin on his face.

'He's up to something,' thought Mikey, and he giggled to himself.

All the team were gathered together, everyone on time. Things were taking shape. Everyone was busy—except one person, Annie. Annie was in charge of the tuck shop. 'This rain is going to spoil the day. Maybe we should postpone it for another day,' she was saying to everyone she met. The team's heart began to sink. However, Mikey took control of the situation. Looking Annie straight in the eye, he told her that her words were bringing down the morale of the team, and for that reason, pointing the finger at her, he said in a strong voice, 'You're fired!' Hearing this, the rest of the team pulled harder together, and in no time at all, everything was in place.

Unexpectedly, the rain stopped, and out of nowhere, the sun shone. It shone so brightly that it was like being in another country. Soon everybody stripped themselves of their rain gear. The sun was shining; the stage was set. Positively, God is smiling down at us,' thought Mikey.

Soon the whole place was filled with people sitting and standing. Mikey got up on the stage and took the mike. The crowd let out a big roar and clapped their hands. The show would soon start. Mikey thanked everyone for coming. What a joy to see so many faces. Mikey noticed that little Tilly was in the crowd. Tilly, although poor in health, had sold the most tickets, and Mikey wanted to make this known to the people. The people gave Tilly the biggest clap ever heard for anyone. Wazer opened the show with a special song for Tilly, which he made himself. The audience was spellbound to see such a little lad with such a big voice. He was so talented that there was not a dry eye in the place.

Freddy and his band, Rat-a-tat-tats, gave a great performance. Hands were waving; the crowd was singing. There were people tapping their feet and people dancing on the street. While the spirits of the people were high, Freddy and his friends took the opportunity to sing for all the needy children in the whole world, especially in Africa, where they had no food. 'Feed the wo-rl-d, don't you know they have no fo-od? Feed the wo-rl-d . . .'

The next group to perform was Jes. They were a big hit. The crowd cheered. It was obvious to see that they had brought rays of sunshine to both young and old.

Mikey announced that before the break, the twins Mar and Mite would perform. As they walked on the stage, screeches of pure joy could be heard from all the children in the audience. Girls ran up to the front of the stage, blowing kisses at the twin boys. The children who had been in the hospital gave three 'Hip, hip, hooray' cheers to the twins, who took the time to visit them. 'Hip, hip, hooray!' they cheered louder and louder.

Everyone was thirsty. The tuck shop made a lot of profit. The cakes of Jamie's mum went down a treat. Jamie's photos were on display, and the laughter and the giggles could be heard from miles away.

Mikey's uncle opened the second half of the concert. 'Look to the sky,' he says. 'There is a big surprise coming. We don't know the time but keep on looking up.'

The Five Alive group came on stage; however, all five were going in different directions. This aggravated Elizabeth so much so that she shouted in a loud voice, 'Excuse me, excuse me, would you five boys please go in one direction.' This caused an uproar of laughter among the audience.

'Look, look to the sky. He is coming,' shouted a young child. Not many people took notice of the young child. They were so busy laughing and having fun that they didn't see the parachute in the sky and missed the landing. The young soldier got up from the ground, dusted off his uniform, ran his fingers through his dashing red hair, winked at the ladies, and walked over to his friend, Uncle Philip.

Uncle Philip introduced the young man. 'This is Prince. We call him Prince at the barracks because he can dance like Michael Jackson.' Prince captivated the audience with his unique style of dancing. It was a mixture of break, crip walk, and jump style. He loved to party, and when he finished his act, people—young and old alike—were queuing for his autograph.

Mikey noticed a young man in the shadows. It was Webster. 'Come up and do your party piece,' yelled Mikey at him. Webster came out of the shadows, took the mike, and stood alone. The music started, and Webster sang a melody of songs. He had the whole audience up their hands in the air, singing, 'YMCA, YMCA.' He finished with the song 'Congratulations and Celebrations'. The whole event had been an awesome success. 'Congratulations and jubilations, we want the world to be a happier place to live.'

Last but not least was Mikey and Mudsy. Mikey took to the stage and was very nervous. He had never done anything like this before. His heart was beating fast. Suddenly he saw her there, sitting on the front row. He could never mistake that face. 'I'll make her so proud of me,' he thought. Elizabeth introduced the double act. 'And here is our final act of the day. Give a great, big hand for Mopsy and Mudsy.' The duo danced and performed in a way that they got a standing ovation. The crowd clapped and cried, 'More, more.' But one person stood up and clapped until her hands hurt. She was so proud of her boy. 'My beautiful, special son,' she thought. Elizabeth was so proud of them both as well. She was sure that Mikey and Mudsy did the whole performance for her. Did their eyes not lock together on a number of occasions? Yes, she was sure—very sure.

Elizabeth closed the show and reminded everyone to pick up their rubbish and to bring it home with them. Elizabeth was very proud of her country and did not want any litter spoiling the beautiful countryside.

That night, Mikey lay on his bed, too flabbergasted to sleep at the generosity of the people. He would make plans to distribute the fund-raising money. He was certain that the children in need would benefit from their hard work. He would do it on Monday, for tomorrow he would rest. *Zzzzzzzz.*

The profits from this book will go to Project Playground International.

In September 2015 a team from Forces Regroup and Elim Christian Life Centre (CLC) based in Cheshire UK will travel to Romania to build a playground for House of Dreams in Chicerea near Iasi.

Forces Regroup are ex-soldier personnel who are suffering from Post- Traumatic Stress Disorder (PTSD). On leaving the army many soldiers cannot forget the sights of suffering of the innocent especially children. By doing this project they believe it will bring healing to their inward wounds and happiness to many underprivileged children in the world.

House of Dreams Romania is a respite home for many children living in orphanages in Romania. The children themselves called it the House of Dreams as many long to be living in a normal home. This house provides a holiday for the children who otherwise would not know anything else other than the orphanage surroundings. This playground is very much needed for the children to have a safe area to play.

Drawings by Daniel Maxwell

If you would like to donate to help build a playground in Iasi Romania you can do so at;

NatWest
Po Box 65
International Helps Project
Account number
40861108
Sort code
01-05-41

Lightning Source UK Ltd.
Milton Keynes UK
UKOW03f0337121014

239962UK00004B/255/P